Angela Anaconda™

Teacher Trouble

POCKET
BOOKS

Based on the TV series *Angela Anaconda*® created by Joanna Ferrone and Sue Rose as seen on Channel 4

POCKET
B O O K S

First published in 2001 by Simon & Schuster Inc.
This revised edition first published in 2001 by Pocket Books with new illustrations
An imprint of Simon & Schuster UK Limited
Africa House, 64-78 Kingsway, London WC2B 6AH

© 2001 DECODE Entertainment, Inc.
Copyright in *Angela Anaconda* and all related characters is owned by
DECODE Entertainment Inc.
ANGELA ANACONDA is a registered trademark of Honest Art, Inc. All Rights Reserved.

Design & imaging by Threefold Ltd ©Simon & Schuster UK Ltd

POCKET BOOKS and colophon are registered trademarks of Simon & Schuster.
A CIP catalogue record for this book is available from the British library.

ISBN 07434 15809

1 3 5 7 9 10 8 6 4 2

Printed in Hong Kong by Midas

CONTENTS

You're So Vain

Chapter 1

Hello, in case you don't know this already, my name is Angela Anaconda, and I want to tell you about something terrible that happened to me in school one day that was not my fault.

At all. It was just another boring day in my third-grade classroom at Tapwater Springs Elementary.

Mrs Brinks, our teacher, who is mean to everyone except Miss Teacher's Pet, Ninnie Wart Manoir (otherwise known as Nanette), told us we had to write a rhyming poem about someone we really admire.

Of course, Nanette wanted to know if we could put French words in our poems. Why, you ask? Because Nanette Manoir, who is *not* French, wants everybody to think she *is* French, even though she is *not*. And since Mrs Brinks has never said the word "NO" (which rhymes with THROW, as in throw up), Nanette is allowed to use French in her poem. But who cares, because how was I supposed to know this was the assignment that was about to ruin my whole life?

On the way home from school that day, with my best friends Gina Lash and Johnny Abatti, I thought of everybody who was important to me. Then Gina Lash said, "You'll never guess who I've picked, Angela Anaconda. It's Tiny Dottie, the snack food czar. She's a successful entrepreneur and she makes a darn good cream cake. Just think of the research *I'll* get to do!"

You see, Gina Lash loves to eat, and what she loves to eat the most is Tiny Dottie cakes, especially those pink coconut snowballs. She can eat fourteen in one day. But what I would like to know is, how come Tiny Dottie is so tiny if her cakes are so darn good?

Then Johnny Abatti says he is going to write about his Uncle Nicky. "He's the best! He hardly ever went to school, and he never goes to work, and he drives real fast, too!"

"Of course he does," says Gina Lash. "That's because he's always being chased by the police." So, anyway, then it is my turn to tell, and I tell my friends they are just going to have to guess who I'm picking because I am not telling. And even Gina Lash, the smartest in class, can't guess.

"Why don't you just tell us?" she and Johnny ask me.

"Because it's a secret," I tell them. "And if I tell, it won't be a secret any more. Even *I* know that."

"But we told you who we admire most."

"Sorry, Johnny and Gina," I tell them. "A surprise is a surprise on account of it's a surprise." And then we got to my house where I live and I waved good-bye to my friends.

"See you later when you see me!" I tell them.

Like I said, Johnny and Gina are my best friends except for one friend who is an even *better* best friend – the best friend anybody could ever have! Can you guess who that is? It's who comes to greet me on my front walk and almost knocks me over and licks my face every day: my pet dog, King!

"Hello, King," I say. "How's my girl, the best dog in the entire world?" And when we run into the house I cannot wait to tell King all about my new assignment. "We have to write a poem about someone we admire enough to write a poem about, and nobody picked as good a pick as mine!" I tell her.

So, we walk into the kitchen, and there's my mum: "Hi, sweetie, I've made chocolate chips, but no cookies till you wash your hands," she tells me, even though they look perfectly clean to me and I don't get or see how cookies could make my hands dirty. "Oh, brother," I say to myself, except whenever I say something to myself, my mother can always seem to hear it from ten miles away. See, my mum might be really nice for a mother, and I like her a lot and wouldn't want a different one, but sometimes she drives me crazy.

"March!" she tells me.

While I'm in the bathroom washing my hands, I tell King all about my project.

"The someone I am writing about looks out for everyone in my family, and when I grow up, I want to be just like her!" I explain. Then I notice that King must be thirsty, because she's doing something truly gross: she's drinking from the toilet bowl. "Well, except for the drinking from the toilet thing," I tell her. "Can you guess who it is, girl?" Because she is so smart, King answers with a bark. "You're right. It's you, King!"

So that night I work very hard on writing my poem, and I cannot wait to get to school tomorrow.

CHAPTER 2

The next day at school Johnny and Gina can't wait to know who I picked, but I still will not tell them. Josephine Praline, who loves religion, goes first, and she wrote a poem about a nun who was burned at the stake. *That* made everyone quiet. Then Mrs Big Mouth Brinks gets up and asks her favourite pet, Nanette Manoir, to go next. I can see Johnny and Gina turn red. They know for sure that Nanette Manoir is not going to stop talking for ten hours at least and they want to know who I picked and this will make them have to wait.

When Miss Nanny-goat herself stands up, there is a lot of oohing and aahing from her Copycat-Clone-Club, January and Karlene. "Why, Nanette," says Mrs Brinks (like she was in love), "what a pretty new frock you have on!"

"*Merci beaucoup*, Mrs Brinks," says creepy Nin. "It's a

11

Paris original in honour of the person I have chosen for my poem: Marie Antoinette, the famous queen of France." Not only does Nanette have a superfancy shiny dress on, she also has a giant picture of that queen who wanted everyone to eat cake, so they cut her head off.

Anyway, Nanette starts torturing us with her poem, when a miracle happens and Nanumbskull sits back down again! "I'm sorry, Mrs Brinks," she says, "but I was planning to use the recess period to perfect the delivery of my lengthy poem about royalty. Perhaps Angela, who undoubtedly has written something substantially shorter, should go first."

Then those clone drone friends of hers, January and Karlene, start to laugh, and since Mrs Brinks always agrees with everything that comes out of Nanette Manoir's un-French mouth, she says, "How considerate of you, Nanette!"

Then it was a dream come true for Johnny and Gina. Mrs Brinks tells me to stand up and read my poem first.

CHapter 3

Before beginning I decided to say a few words as an introduction: "Even though some kids picked someone *famous* to write about, I decided to write about someone I truly admire. Someone I learn from every day." All of a sudden even Mrs Brinks is interested. "Okay, here goes," I say. Since I'm never used to all that attention, I then clear my throat and begin:

> "You have perfect manners,
> You never drool.
> You even help me get through school.
> You're playful and friendly,
> You're open and brave.
> It's you who teaches me how to behave.
> In the garden beds where you usually go,
> It seems to help the flowers grow.

Even your little whiskers are neat
And the fuzzy fur upon your feet.
Your hair is so beautiful,
You don't need to wear clothes,
You're devoted and loyal,
And I like your cold, wet nose.
You're the very best role model I've ever met.
It is I who should be *your* pet. The end."

In my entire year in this classroom I have never done as well as now! Mrs Brinks is actually crying! At first I think it is because I said something wrong, but the real reason is that she is so happy. "Miss Anaconda, I never knew," she said. "You have the makings of the next Emily Dickinson!"

(Whoever *that* is.)

Even though Johnny and Gina look a little annoyed, I figure it is because they are so jealous. And if Ninnie Wart's brain was not so damp and soggy, there would have been steam coming out of her ears. "Don't worry, Nanette," says her clone friend

14

January, "I'm sure your poem is much better than hers."

And by the look on Dim Nin's face, I can tell it is not.

Up until that point I am the happiest I will ever be in that class. Then Mrs Brinks says something that ruins everything. "Well, Miss Anaconda, you could've knocked me down with a feather. I had no idea you felt this way about me!"

What did she say? All of a sudden everything that was so good is now so bad. I try to tell Mrs Brinks that the poem is really about King and definitely not about her, but I can't speak and she keeps making things worse by getting happier and happier. Then she decides that she wants me to write my poem out on the blackboard for the whole school to see. Things get more terrible when Nanette and her dumb duet are leaving for recess and I'm still stuck writing on the board.

"At least I'm not a brown-noser like Angela Anaconda," says Nanette. *"Your beautiful hair, your lovely gaze. Since I wrote this poem, I get straight A's."*

You know what the worst part is? Even if I did write that poem about Mrs Brinks like everyone thought I did, then I would hate me even more than Nanette does.

CHAPTER 4

Out on the playground that day it's terrible. Johnny Abatti and Gina Lash act like they hardly even know me. All the other kids are whispering about me. Finally I catch up to Johnny and Gina on the swings and Johnny is so surprised, he can't keep quiet any longer. "Mrs Brinks? Since when did you start liking *her*?" he asks.

"Come on, Johnny and Gina," I tell them. "You know I wouldn't write a poem like that about Mrs Brinks. I wrote it about KING!"

Both of them get very confused.

"As in Martin Luther King?" asks Gina.

17

"Or Elvis?" asks Johnny.

"Not THE King," I say. "My dog, King!" At first I didn't think either one of them really believed me. "I knew I should've left in that part about 'drinking from the toilet'."

Then Gina Lash finally looks in my face, which was very upset, and says, "Angela Anaconda, you are really in a pickle."

"I tried to tell Mrs Brinks," I explain. Then Gina says never, ever, under any circumstance tell Mrs Brinks. And she doesn't even have to tell me that, on account of I know how mad Mrs Brinks would get at me if she found out that poem was really written about my dog.

Then creepy Karlene comes over and says, "Look, it's Angela Ana-butt-kisser." And then her creepy Goldilocks boss says something insulting to me in her supposed French, which I know is not French because she is not French and does not speak French.

And Johnny, who is trying to help me out, says, "Angela didn't write that poem about Mrs Brinks! She wrote it about her dog!"

If you gave Nanette Manoir a real French fry at that moment, she would not have been happier. "Oh, she did, did

she?" Nanette says as she walks away with a nasty grin on her un-French face.

That's when Gina Lash and I know that not only am I dead but I am buried, too.

Chapter 5

Back in the classroom, Mrs Brinks is still smiling at me like I am her favourite, which is what I have become. She makes me sit in the desk up front and moves Ninnie Wart to the back. I cannot even enjoy that moment because first of all, Nanette is not even mad, and second of all, Nanette is raising her hand. "Mrs Brinks?" she says. "About Angela's lovely poem . . ."

Uh-oh, here it comes, I think. And I am right.

When Ninny tells her who I have written my poem about, Mrs Brinks not only turns as red as a fire engine, she screeches like one too. "HER DOG?" she screams. Then she starts looking at my poem as if it were a list of personal insults against her, and the whole class starts laughing and barking like dogs.

"Mrs Brinks, I tried to tell you," I say.

"SILENCE!" Mrs Brinks screams. Then she makes me

take an eraser and erase the poem she once loved off the blackboard. As I am doing that I start wishing I had written a much shorter poem, because it feels like it is taking forever. "After you get rid of that abomination, Miss Anaconda," says Mrs Brinks (she was not done with me yet), "I want you to go outside and clap every trace of chalk off those erasers!"

The only good part of that job (which I hate more than anything, by the way) is that I did not have to hear the world's biggest teacher's pet get up and read her French queen poem, which I knew would surely take forever.

As I was clapping those erasers and wishing I could redecorate Miss Ninnie Poo's fancy un-French dress, I started thinking up a new poem. . .

What if Mrs Brinks was none other than
Queen Marie Antoinette herself, with a big
white wig and her pet Nanette bowing before
her? I thought to myself:

Oh, little Nin, I must proclaim,
Your poem about that queen was lame.
And you, Mrs Brinks, with your head so big,
Your nose is running, and your hair is a wig!

And then what if when Mrs Brinks blows her
nose, her wig shoots up and lands sideways on her
head? Then King and I would come in with crowns
on our heads and we would take those horrible two
to the land of their dreams!

Come Ninny and Brinksy to land in Paree,
Where my dog King and me
Make all the rules to which you must agree.
My dearest of teachers and your favourite pet,
Please don't you worry and, geez, don't you fret.

And then what if Uncle Nicky, who drives his Corvette way too fast, pulls up and none other than Gina Lash steps out of the front seat, carrying a tray of her all-time favourite Tiny Dottie snack cakes? Just as Brinks and Nin are going to the guillotine, of all places.

For here is Gina come to serve
You little cakes you don't deserve.
Oh, naughty, nonnie, prissy miss
And Marie Antoi-Brinks, whose butt you kiss.
Let's see how you cackle when canine King tackles
The difficult chore –
You insufferable bores –
Of sentencing you
To a swirlie for two.

And then, just when they think their heads will come off, Brinks and Nin instead realize that they must suffer a fate worse than death: Cleaning King's toilet!

"We beg you for mercy," you'll pathetically cry.

"Oh, greatest of queens, ten times smarter than I."

"But, Angela, save us!"

You'll snivel and snort.

"Don't be outrageous," I'll kindly retort.

Scrub little Ninnie, you too, Mrs Brinks.

The King can't have germs

In the water she drinks.

And because poor Nanette hates scrubbing King's toilet so much, I can hear her screaming, "AAAAAAAH."

Just then I stop clapping my erasers and realize that Nanette Manoir really *is* screaming in real life for real. And she is standing right next to me. "SNAP OUT OF IT!" she screams. It is as if she can tell what I am thinking about.

"Mrs Brinks sent me out to get you, but look at you now. You're all white, covered in that filthy chalk dust. You look like my DOG!"

"So sorry, Nanette, I was lost in a FOG."

You see, even though this was one of the most horrible days of my life, I still found out that poetry is kind of fun. And

I also found out that I'm actually kinda good at it.

"Let's go back inside before the sun damages my fine silk ATTIRE," said Nanette.

"After you, Ninnie-Poo, who I've always ADMIRED." I hate to admit it, but I was having fun outside with my poems and ideas. And since Nanette Manoir is the official teacher's pet, and because she said Mrs Brinks wanted me inside, I figured I had to follow her. . .

Oops, was that *my* chalk handprint on the back of Ninnie's favourite silk dress?

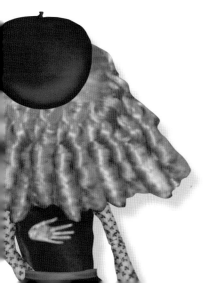

THE SUBSTITUTE

CHAPTER 1

It is no big surprise that breakfast is the worst meal of the day in my house where I live. Why? You might ask. Well, as much as I hate to give them any attention, my two dimwit brothers, Derek and Mark, take all the delicious candy fruit out of the fruity flakes cereal, leaving me with only the flakes, which you might as well buy as plain fruitless flakes because they are boring and have no taste.

Derek and Mark (or "Dork" and "Mork," as I like to call them) also take all the milk, which makes the plain cornflakes even more horrible and impossible to eat. Then Baby Lulu, who I secretly think is on the side of the dimwits, usually spills her bottle all over me *and* my homework, and I am just lucky I have my dog King to lick it up.

But what made this morning even more bad than ever was that I was supposed to think up what I was doing for my rain forest project and by the time I finished fighting with my brothers and getting squirted by Baby Lulu, I did not. So when I got to my third-grade class at Tapwater Springs Elementary School, I expected my teacher, Mrs Brinks, to get mad because I did not have a thought in my head about the rain forest, much less a project about the rain forest. But then, instead of things being really bad, all of a sudden things started to get really good.

First, when we got to our classroom, Mrs Brinks was not there, which was good sign number one. Then, the principal made an announcement and said that Mrs Brinks was sick and we would be getting a substitute teacher.

As if you didn't know, the only one who was not cheering was Miss Do-Nothing Class Monitor Teacher's Pet Rat,

Nanette Manoir, who had worn her endangered species
crocodile shoes as a visual example of her rain forest subject.
Then Johnny Abatti gets the idea to make paper aeroplanes
out of our maths homework, and guess what? Mine flew
much better than his! A lot better. So well that it hit the lady
with short hair and glasses who was coming into the room.
Our substitute teacher. Oh, no, I am finished before she even
starts, I thought to myself. But that's when really good thing
number two happened.

"Anyone here named Angela?" she asked as she read my
name off the maths homework that was now a paper
aeroplane.

"That's Angela, there!" said Johnny Abatti, who was not being mean or trying to get me in trouble like Ninnie Wart would, but who was just being Johnny, who is not that smart.

"Uh-oh," said Gina Lash, who is my best friend and who *is* very smart.

Instead of getting mad or making me go to the principal's office as Mrs Brinks would if she got hit with my maths homework (which was turned into a paper aeroplane), this lady fixed the wing on my plane and flew it right back to me! If only you could've seen the look on Nanette Manoir's un-French face and on the faces of her clone drone friends January and Karlene!

Chapter 2

Then the substitute teacher said her name was Geraldine Klump. "But you can call me Geri." Like she was a friend of ours, like Johnny or Gina or Angela (me!). I don't know about you, but mostly when we have a substitute, our class does not listen, and instead of getting schoolwork done, we get nothing done. But that never stops Nanette Manoir from trying to be the goody-goody boss of all time.

"Miss Klump," said Nanette to Geri, not calling her Geri like she asked us to. "I feel it is my academic duty to go over our homework assignment from last night, and I am fully prepared to discuss the topic of my rain forest project, which is 'The Scandalous Shortage of the Crocodile'."

"Endangered species, now that's a topic a girl could sink her teeth into," said Geri. Uh-oh, was she starting to make our little Na-nutski *her* pet too?

33

But I shouldn't have been so worried, because when Nanette explained to Geri that the theme of her project wasn't about the crocodiles themselves (which she didn't care about), but only that there were not enough crocodile pocketbooks or shoes in the world on account of the international trade bans, Geri got really mad. "Young lady," she said. "*That's* not a project. That's a peck full of poppycock!"

Was that Nanette Manoir she was talking to? No one in the class could believe it. Least of all, Nanette and her copycat twin Nins, January and Karlene.

"Do you think she's really a teacher?" asked Gina Lash. Because who ever heard of a substitute teacher you actually liked?

Chapter 3

Later that day in the cafeteria I was a little jealous of Johnny and Gina because they each had thought of good rain forest projects. Gina was writing about "Amazon Crunch", that peanut and raisin mix you can buy at the grocery store, and Johnny was writing about cannibals. And even though I was not at home getting milk spilled on me and having my cereal ruined by those caveman leftovers from the Stone Age, Derek and Mark, I still could not think of a good enough project.

That's when good thing number three happened.

"Hey, Angela, is this seat taken?" It was Geri and she wanted to sit with us!

At first I was surprised. "Are you talking to me?" I asked. Teachers never know your name on the first day of teaching.

"Never forget a face full of freckles," she said, as she sat down right next to me, Gina and Johnny! And you know what? She told me she had freckles just like me when she was a kid!

"Yoo-hoo, Miss Klump! There's plenty of room over here at the popular kids' table!" said the voice of Nanette Manoir, which could kill a crocodile just by its horrible sound alone.

"Fine right here, Janet," said Geri with a wave of her hand like Nanette did not matter at all.

"It's *Nan*ette!" corrected Little Nin. But Geri did not care, she was too busy opening up the scary-looking sandwich that they call lunch at our school.

"Wish we had some pizza," said Geri. "I've had better meals cooked by headhunters."

"Wow!" said Johnny Abatti. "You know real, live headhunters?"

"Sure," said Geri. And she showed us pictures of herself in the actual rain forest with actual rain forest hunters with spears and necklaces made of teeth.

"Look at those houses the headhunters live in," I said. "They look exactly like the tree house Johnny and I built!"

"Hey, that's a great idea for your rain forest project!" Geri said, easy as pie. And she gave me the picture for me to keep. What a great day this was turning out to be – not only did I have a teacher who actually liked me and not Nanette Manoir, but I had a project to do that I actually wanted to do!

At home I decided that the only way my brother Derek could pay me back for ruining every breakfast of my entire life was to let me borrow his Popsicle stick collection to build my rain forest project. Of course I was not going to *tell* him that I was borrowing it because I knew he would never let me have it if I asked him for it.

After a messy start with King, the best dog in all the world, who got the sticks glued to her fur, and me, who got the sticks glued to my fingers, I built a real model of an actual headhunter's house. Just like in Geri's picture.

I couldn't wait to take it to school the next day, where I knew everyone would be thrilled and amazed. The only thing left that my house needed was a roof of straw. The straw was not even a problem to get, because I was able to take it out of Scamp our pet hamster's cage, and I'm sure he didn't even miss it.

Chapter 4

The next day in the schoolyard Gina Lash was the first one to get excited when I held up my model of my Amazon headhunter's house.

"Just think," she said. "Someone ate all those Popsicles!"

"Just be careful not to touch it," I said. "It's still a little wet."

Now, I don't know what it is about Johnny Abatti, but sometimes he does exactly what you ask him not to do. And it's not because he is mean like a certain baloney-headed girl I know, or because he can't hear so great or because he only uses half his brain. He is just being Johnny, but as soon as I said "don't touch it," Johnny goes and gets his finger stuck to my house. Things might've turned out fine, but before Gina Lash and I could figure out how to get Johnny's finger unstuck so that my house would be okay, Ninnie Wart and her dummy duet come strolling along to make sure that things would not turn out fine at all.

"EEW!" said the Nannoying one. "A house of germs from Popsicle sticks that have been in other people's mouths! Let's get out of here. Coming, John?" As her putrid pals were yelling, "Gross!", Nanette yanked Johnny's arm and since he was still stuck to my house, it got smashed to smithereens.

"You've broken my stilt house that is now completely ruined!" I was almost crying. "Now it looks like I didn't even *do* my project!"

"Don't worry, Angela," said Gina Lash. "Geri will let you fix it. It's not as if you have to take that mess to Mrs Brinks."

"She'd throw *that* right in the garbage," said Johnny.

And I knew that they were right, so I was feeling a lot better when I went into the classroom.

Why is it that just when you are sure things are going to turn out good they always end up turning out worse than you ever thought possible? Why is it that Mrs Brinks is not our substitute teacher and Geri is not our real teacher? Why is it that when I brought my broken house into class, which I was all set to fix, Mrs Brinks was standing there and not Geri?

"Angela Anaconda, what is that mess you are dropping everywhere?" Mrs Brinks asked.

"Oh, Mrs Brinks," said the Dizzy Nanizzy. "Too bad the joyous occasion of your return has been marred by all this gluey debris!"

"That's not debris, that's my rain forest project," I tried to explain. But I knew Mrs Brinks would never understand.

"Very funny, young lady," she said. "Now clean up this mess immediately!"

And that's how I ended up having to go to the janitor's closet to get a bucket of water and wishing I could mop the floor with Ninny Poo's golden baloney curls.

CHapTeR 5

As I was running the water I started thinking about the rain forest and how at first I didn't like the stupid homework project, and how along came Geri and then I loved it and now I couldn't care less if I never heard the words "rain forest" again.

I could see Mrs Brinks and her precious Nanette (which rhymes with pet) playing croquet in their crocodile shoes while I, Angela Anaconda, officially welcomed them to the real rain forest. The rain forest where it really rains. Then I would pound out all my messages on the drum, warning all my little native friends to seek higher ground in order to escape the torrential downpours.

But what's this? Who's sitting under their sun umbrella while the rain is pouring down all around them? Why, it's Little Nin and Mrs Brinks, who do not speak drum, so they cannot understand my warning. They are too busy trying to speak French, which they don't really know, either. Then, as the river overflows, they try to get on the roof of their hut but they can't. That's when they start to yell and plead with me.

"Angela, Angela, save us!" they will tell me. "This raging river is ruining our crocodile cha-cha shoes!" I, of course, have climbed up on the top of my drum and am waiting for my friends in high places to arrive. And then Geri, the good teacher who knows the real rain forest, will swing in on a vine and carry me to a real amazon tree house made of authentic Popsicle sticks.

As we watch Mrs Brinks and Nanette twirling and screaming down the river, we realize that there is not much we can do to save them. Their only hope is if the relatives of the crocodiles that they have used for shoes decide to help them. And as Mrs Brinks and Nanette head straight for the most treacherous waterfall on earth, Geri and I realize our friends are in danger. We then heroically swing on vines and rescue them – the most endangered of all species – our friends the crocodiles. It is amazing, but at that point I can almost hear Mrs Brinks screaming, "ANGELAAA!" as she goes over the waterfall.

Suddenly I can actually feel the water on my feet too. And I can clearly hear Mrs Brinks screaming, "Have you gone completely hooey?" I must have been day-dreaming, because as I look down I see I am completely flooding the floor in the janitor's closet by letting the water run over the sink.

"After you mop up this mess, take yourself straight to the principal's office!" screams Mrs Brinks.

Just great, I think, what else can go wrong now? I thought yesterday would be a bad day at school and it was the best day ever. Today I came to school with a project I really liked, to see a teacher I really liked, and now I not only have a project that no one likes, but I have a teacher I really don't like, and who really doesn't like me because she loves Nanette Manoir better than anyone. And not only that, but now I am on my way to the principal's office, which only happens when you are in the biggest trouble.

Having a substitute teacher that we all liked (except for Nanoozy and her crowd) was a big surprise. Having Mrs Brinks return to school today was another surprise. But going to the principal's office was the biggest surprise of all. As I was standing in the doorway, the big chair spun around and I was all set to get yelled at when I couldn't believe my eyes!

"Geri?!"

"Hello, Angela! Today I'm substituting for the principal, who's sick. Probably from eating that cafeteria food. Grab a chair! Whadya say we order a pizza for lunch?"

Geri, the only *teacher* who was ever nice to me, was now the only *principal* who was ever nice to me. Over pizza I told

Geri all about the rain forest house I built out of Popsicle sticks and how I flooded the janitor's closet. She said she thought it would be a good time to ask Mrs Brinks and her perfect class monitor Annette to clean out the janitor's closet.

"It's Nanette," I said.

"Right," she winked. "And since Mrs Brinks and Annette will be so busy today, how about we go and join the rest of your class out on the playground for what's left of the day."

TOUCHED BY AN ANGEL-a

Chapter 1

In case you think that I have never tried to be nice to Nanette Manoir, let me tell you that I *have* tried. But she is not easy to be nice to, on account of the fact that she is not nice.

Ask Josephine Praline, who is training to become a saint and who says she sees good in everybody – even Nanette. She will tell you about the time she tried to make me see some good in Nanette too.

It all began during nature science. Me and

51

my friends and a certain person I just mentioned, who is mean and not nice to anyone, are learning about caves.

"So, remember, children," says my teacher, Mrs Brinks, "stalactites hang tightly while stalagmites stand mightily!" She points to the picture of the cave. "Have you ever seen anything as impressive as those stalactites?"

Johnny Abatti, my dim-witted friend, points at the ceiling. "You mean more impressive than Uncle Nicky's Eternal Spitball?" he asks. Johnny's Uncle Nicky is famous. And Uncle Nicky's Eternal Spitball that has been hanging like a stalactite from the ceiling of our classroom since before I even was born is even more famous than Uncle Nicky himself.

We all look up and stare at it. Johnny Abatti turns around in his seat. "Uncle Nicky used to eat paste, so it's never coming down," he tells us.

"I hope you're wrong as usual, John," says Nanette Manoir. "The sooner that hideous aberration of school property that you and a *certain* tasteless person whose initials are AA –" and she looks right at me – "call a 'spitball' comes down from that ceiling the better."

"You mean the sooner you're allergic to your own brain the better, Nanette Manure," I whisper to Johnny.

But Josephine Praline must have heard me. "Angela Anaconda," she says nervously in that quiet way of hers. "You must confess, that wasn't a very nice thing to say. If you harbour such feelings in your heart, you'll never be touched by an angel. And if you're never touched by an angel, your life will be nothing but trouble."

I roll my eyes. "Sure, Josephine Praline, whatever you say," I reply. Besides, who needs to be touched by an angel, anyway, I think to myself.

But then some strange things start to happen. Because the next thing I know – YUCK! – the Eternal Spitball that was supposed to be eternally attached to the ceiling falls right onto my desk! And not onto Johnny's desk or Gina's desk or anyone else's desk but onto *my* desk, mine!

"Hallelujah!" cries Josephine Praline. "It's a sign from Above!"

But Mrs Brinks does not think that it is a sign from Above. She thinks it is a sign that I have done something I wasn't supposed to do. Which is not fair, because I haven't done any such thing. A giant shadow shaped like a refrigerator with a waistline falls over my desk. I look up to see Mrs Brinks's angry face. "Dispose of your repugnant handiwork at once!" she yells at me.

"But I didn't do anything!" I protest. "It's Uncle Nicky's!"

"Don't be ridiculous," she tells me. On account of Uncle Nicky had dropped out of Tapwater Springs Elementary about twenty-five years ago, I get sent to clean the chalkboard erasers. When I stand up to go, Josephine Praline whispers to me, "That wouldn't have happened if you had been touched by an angel."

Chapter 2

But I am still not so sure about needing an angel to touch me. Even though the next thing that happens to me should have been pretty convincing.

"The spitball was not a sign from Above," I have just finished saying to Gina Lash and Johnny Abatti as I brush the chalk dust off and walk onto the playground. "It was an accident!" And just when I say it, a football hits me from behind.

"That was just an accident too!" I say, picking myself up.

But accidents just keep happening to me all day for the rest of the day. Like getting knocked down at the swing. And then my lunch bag breaks, and my sandwich falls on the ground. And somebody steps right on it.

Then Gina Lash says – as if I didn't notice this myself –

"Angela, there's a footprint on your sandwich!"

"Accidents happen," I reply – just before getting splashed by a mud puddle.

"What a recess!" I say to myself in the washroom while I am washing off all of the mud. "If I didn't know better, I'd say I was jinxed!"

"You're not jinxed, Angela Anaconda," says a voice. "You just need an angel."

I look up on account of I think it may be a voice from Heaven. But no one is there. So I look down. And I see someone's shoes in one of the stalls. "Josephine Praline?" I say. "Is that you?"

"Yes, my child, I am with you. And your guardian angel would be too, if you could learn to love your enemies."

"Sure, sure," I say, still not believing her . . . until the tap breaks on the sink, which it has never done, and water sprays all over the place – and Mrs Brinks walks in right when it happens.

"What in the name of Lady Godiva!" she exclaims, looking at all the water. "Angela Anaconda, I think you know what this means."

I guess you know what it means too. I have to go clap more of Mrs Brinks's erasers, which I have already clapped a million times. But, anyway, I clap those erasers as hard as I can.

And then there is a white cloud of white chalk dust and I might think I am seeing things, but I really do see Josephine Praline drift by like a ghost with a little, tiny teeny angel on her shoulder.

"Hey, Josephine!" I call. "Wait up!" On account of I am starting to think that maybe she is right after all. Maybe I really do need an angel.

Chapter 3

So that is it. I finally decide that maybe I'd better try to act nice to everyone. Because I sure need a guardian angel, big-time. I go back into the washroom and I stand up on the toilet seat so I can talk about this to Josephine, who is still in the next stall.

"If you want to be touched by an angel, you have to learn to be kind and good. And you must learn to love your enemies," she says.

"Okay." I shrug.

"*Even* your Nanettes," she says firmly.

"On second thoughts," I say, "maybe I could just get a rabbit's foot," and right then I fall into the toilet. Which means it is definitely time to act nice – even to Nanette.

In the cafeteria, I tell Gina Lash and Johnny Abatti that I plan to try to be nice to Nanette. They can hardly believe their own ears.

"You hafta do what?" asks Johnny Abatti.

"You heard me," I say. "I have to be nice to Ninnie Wart. Otherwise I'm doomed to a life of trouble my whole life."

And then I hear Ninnie-Poo, who is sitting a few tables away, say, "Oh, poo! Cook forgot to remove the crusts on my cucumber sandwich again!"

This is my chance to try to be nice to my enemy. Only I can't just give her my stepped-on sandwich, on account of it was stepped on. So when Johnny Abatti is temporarily blinded by getting sauce in his eye, I grab his plate of spaghetti and bring it over to her table.

"Here you go, Nanette," I say as nice as I can be. "A crust-free lunch just for you."

"*Spaghetti?*" sneers Nanette. "The only pasta that touches *my* lips is angel hair."

I can't help it: This makes me so mad, I imagine pouring the spaghetti right over her perfect baloney curls. That would show her. But instead of that, what really happens is I slip, and Johnny's spaghetti flies out of my hands and lands on me without any curls. Have I tripped? Maybe. But then again . . . maybe not.

"She started it!" I say out loud, so if there is an angel listening it can hear me.

Later that day Josephine Praline comes up with more advice. "Try offering her something she truly *needs,* Angela Anaconda."

Okay, fine, I am thinking, and it starts to rain. So I decide I will share my umbrella with her.

"Angela Anaconda, give me that! You almost put out one of my sparkling eyes!" is what she says. And she grabs *my* umbrella and walks all the way to her house with me running after her like all of a sudden it was her umbrella. She stays dry. I get wet. In my wetness I find it hard to think nice things to think about Nanette. But I tell myself I will keep trying.

The next morning I surprise her by waiting outside her house with another umbrella. Who cares if it isn't even raining any more?

"Hi, Nanette!" I say as nice as possible. "I practised all night and now I know how to hold an umbrella just like they do in France, where you are most certainly from."

I try to hold the umbrella for her so the sun's rays won't damage her sensitive skin. I shield her from the sun all the way to school, but when we get there, all she does is tell Mrs Brinks that I was chasing her with my umbrella.

"I was only trying to act nice," I say.

Josephine Praline shakes her head. "Angela, Angela, it's not enough to *act* nice to Nanette. You have to *be* nice in your heart. Don't lose faith, my child," says Josephine. She tears a piece of paper out of her notebook. "Here. Make a list of all the things that are nice about Nanette. Just find one thing and an angel will find you."

What I'd like to know is: Is Josephine Praline praying for a miracle or something?

CHAPTER 4

So that's how I have ended up sitting in my room, trying to think of just one nice thing to write down about Nanette Manoir. "There is nothing nice about Nanette," I say, staring at the blank piece of paper in front of me. "Think, think, think," I tell myself.

And that's when it happens. I think I see the Angel Josephine and she is floating on a cloud right in front of me in my very own room.

"Take my hand, Angela Anaconda," says the Angel Josephine. *"Together we shall find the Nanette who has been forgotten. The nice Nanette."*

65

So I take her hand, and we fly away out of the window on a cloud and look for the nice Nanette.

The first place we come to is a sandbox. There we can see little baby Nanette and little baby Angela playing together.

"Observe," says Angel Josephine. "Innocence playing."

"Excusez-moi," we hear the little Nanette say to the little Angela. "I'm afraid this zone has been set aside for the construction of a new freeway for my Santa Barbara Susie's new convertible." And Alfredo, her servant, comes along and mooshes little Angela's sand castle, and makes her cry.

"Hmm," says the Angel Josephine, frowning. "Oh well, she's just . . . a baby!"

Next we see Nanette walk into a hospital room. She is dressed like a volunteer worker. "Ah," says Angel Josephine.

"Observe Nanette, merciful and caring."

"What beautiful flowers, Mrs Moran," we hear Nanette say to the old woman lying in the bed. "But seeing as they spoil your view of the parking lot, I'm sure you'd like me to have them." And she takes them from the vase. And poor old Mrs Moran can do nothing, only moan.

Then Angel Josephine starts looking a little like she doesn't like what she sees.

So next we fly to Nanette's bedroom. There she lies sleeping, wearing a fancy silk gown and matching eye covers.

"Ah," says Angel Josephine. "There's nice Nanette. Innocent in her dreams."

Nanette wakes up.

"Hello, Nanette," says Angel Josephine. "I am an angel."

"I really don't care if you're Mother Teresa," says Nanette. "How dare you ruin my beauty sleep! Now scoot, scoot, scoot!"

"But I'm here to show Angela . . ." says Angel Josephine.

"ANGELA? That does it. I'm getting Security."

As she pulls the alarm, we fly out of the window. Angel Josephine turns to me, and she's not looking too happy. "You were right, Angela. There isn't anything *nice* about Nanette."

I sigh. "So now I guess I'll never be touched by an angel."

Angel Josephine shrugs. "It could be worse. You could be just like her!"

Just like her . . . just like her . . . just like . . . hey!

I open my eyes and Angel Josephine is gone and I am sitting in my room. But the good thing is I have finally thought of an idea for my list!

CHAPTER 5

The next morning when I get to school I can't wait to show Josephine my list. "I did it! I did it, Josephine! I actually found a lot of nice things to say about Nanette!"

"I knew you would, my child," says Josephine. She peers at my list and begins to read: "One, she's not a twin . . . two, she doesn't have a clone . . . three, there is only one of her."

Josephine looks up at me. "Well, that's not quite what I had in mind, Angela, but . . . it'll do."

"Does that mean I'll be touched by an angel?" I ask her.

"Perhaps," says Josephine, and she makes that dreamy look where her eyes half disappear up into her head, "perhaps you already have been."

Is that a golden halo around Josephine? It sure looks like one to me. Or maybe it is just the school bell behind her head? I can't be sure.

The bell rings. I start to walk into the school, and a football comes flying straight at me.

But guess what?

It misses!

STORY NUMBER FOUR

HOT BOB
AND CHOCOLATE

CHAPTER 1

Hello in case you didn't know, my name is
Angela Anaconda and there is one thing I am the
best at that no one is better at than me. What I am the
best at in Tapwater Springs Elementary School is Mrs Brinks's
Unscramble the Scrambled Words Flash Card game. It is
suppose to teach us how to make perfect sentences, but I just
think it's fun. And I am very good at it. And very fast. But on
this day I am about to tell you about, I was a little too fast.

After I had to sit through everyone going very slowly and
doing very badly at a game I love and do so well, I raised my

73

hand to remind Mrs Brinks that I never had my turn to go.

"Very well, Angela Anaconda," she said as if she could not stand one more minute of this game.

Mrs Brinks put five cards out and I was all set to break my own record of being the Undisputed Champ of Unscrambling or, in other words, the Undisputed Unscrambling Champ! Here were my five cards:

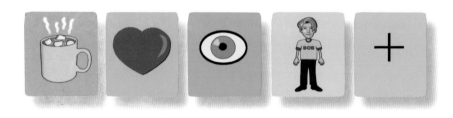

Quick! What do you think this sentence means? I, being champ, had my answer in no time: EYE, PLUS HEART, PLUS BOB, PLUS, HOT CHOCOLATE.

"I love Bob and hot chocolate!" I yelled. Even I was amazed at how fast I unscrambled that one. But like I told you before, sometimes you can be a little too fast.

"Oh you do, do you?" asked Nanette creepy-as-ever Manoir. "Well, who's Bob?"

The rest of the kids in the class started to laugh and I didn't really understand why until Ninnywort said, "I believe the sentence should read: 'Bob and I love hot chocolate'." Or perhaps you're keeping something from us, Angela Anaconda."

Then everyone started to laugh even more. And they started to sing: "Angela and Bob sittin' in a tree, K-I-S-S-I-N-G."

75

If you think I stopped getting teased at lunch and recess –
I didn't. All I heard on the food line and out in the playground
was, "First comes love, then comes marriage, then comes
Angela with a baby carriage."

I ran into the washroom to escape, but on the mirror
someone had written: ANGELA LOVES BOB in lipstick. And
that was just the beginning. Because the next thing I know, I
go to my locker and there taped to the outside is Mrs Brinks's
Bob flashcard staring back at me. And to make matters

worse, Nanette Manoir and her clone drone friends, January
and Karlene, were standing next to me laughing.

"Very funny whoever did this!" I said because I was really
mad. "Enough is enough on account of it has gone on long
enough. So if you don't really mind," I said. "Please just
LEAVE US ALONE!"

Well, it was so quiet all of a sudden that you could have
heard a fly sneeze. Everyone had come in from recess and
now they were all staring at me.

Chapter 2

"**U**s?" asked Nanette. "Who's us?" She wanted to know.

Oh no, I thought, now what did I say? "I mean me!" I said. "Leave me alone!"

"Oh my gosh, there really is a Bob!" said January.

"And they really are in love!" said Karlene.

For the first time everyone believed it. Even my best friend Gina Lash.

"I'm your best friend," she said. "How come you never told me about you and Bob?"

Was this a nightmare come true, or what?

"Because there is no me and Bob," I tried to explain. "Because there is no Bob!" You would think that Gina Lash would realize that this was true. She is the smartest in our class.

But instead, she said: "I'll take your word for it, Angela Anaconda. But if you change your mind and need to talk about you and your one true love, you know where to find me."

"But Gina Lash, I will never be ready to talk about me and my one true love ever, on account of there is no me and my one true love!" I called after her. Then I heard Johnny and Gordy coming down the hall. And Johnny was really mad.

"Bob, Bob, Bob! That's all anybody's talking about!" he said, not realizing that I was standing right there behind the classroom door.

"First loves are always exciting," said Gordy.

"But why Bob?" asked Johnny. "Why not me? I mean – I was friends with her first! Right?"

Then he hit the 'Bob' flashcard on my locker (which I

had forgotten to take off) as if he were jealous. Johnny Abatti, jealous of Bob the flashcard? Most days I wish I were not in school, but this was one day I really wished I weren't in school – BIG TIME!

Then, two things happened that I did not know about. One, Johnny took the flashcard of Bob off of my locker and ripped it up and threw it in my desk. And two, Gordy told Johnny that the quickest way to win someone's heart is with flowers.

I didn't know that those two things had happened and since it had been twenty minutes since anyone had mentioned you-know-who, I started to think that everyone had forgotten all about him, namely Bob. Unfortunately, this was completely not true.

Chapter 3

We were just in the middle of doing perfectly normal things like being quiet and reading books when someone knocked on our classroom door.

"Come in," calls Mrs Brinks and in steps a delivery man with a big bouquet of flowers. For some reason Mrs Brinks thought the flowers were for her so she got all happy.

"Oh, is it Teacher Appreciation Day already?" she asked with a little smile on her face.

Then the delivery guy said something I really wished he did not say: "Flowers for Angela Anaconda!"

Never in my life have I received flowers, or thought about flowers, or wanted to get flowers. Flowers are what ladies in boring movies get. Now not only do I get flowers in front of my whole entire class, but because they are not for Mrs Brinks, she gets very annoyed with me! I would have liked for that bunch of flowers to disappear but all the kids in the class were yelling at me to read the card.

That's when one of golden baloney-head's sidekick's, January, grabs the card and reads it for me: "Me and Angela love hot chocolate," she read.

The room was silent.

"Signed?" asked Ninny's other clone, Karlene.

"Signed nobody," said January.

I guess by now you're glad you're not me. Here I am, being accused of being in love with a Flashcard named Bob who does not exist in real life. And then out of nowhere, I, Angela Anaconda get a big bunch of flowers I never even wanted.

"That Bob is so romantic!" crooned Karlene.

Then I heard Gordy whisper to Johnny and ask him why he didn't sign the card! "I forgot," said Johnny, as he hit himself on the head.

Johnny sent me the flowers? And everybody thought Bob the flashcard sent me the flowers? I couldn't believe how crazy this was getting!

The only good thing about all of this was that it made Nanette mad. She couldn't bear that someone named Bob (who did not exist) was supposedly in love with me and sending me flowers.

Then, another two things happened that I did not know about. First, Nanette ran to the washroom and erased the 'Angela loves Bob' writing on the mirror and changed it to 'Bob loves Nanette'. Then, since she is the only third grader in Tapwater Springs Elementary to carry a portable cell phone, she called her own fancy flower shop to place an order before she came back to class.

After Nanette came back, we were all quiet and doing our important work, when suddenly there is another knock on the classroom door.

85

"Come in," calls Mrs Brinks and in steps another man with an even bigger bouquet of flowers. This time he is also carrying a thermos of hot chocolate. I covered my head so he would not see me. And meanwhile, I could tell, Gina Lash was hoping that delivery was for me so she could have some of the hot chocolate.

"I knew someone would remember Teacher Appreciation Day!" said Mrs Brinks, still thinking the flowers were for her.

"Here we go again," I thought, expecting the worst, as usual. But then the delivery guy said something that surprised us all.

"Flowers and hot chocolate for Nanette Manoir!"

"*Pour moi?*" asked Nanette in her unFrench French, trying to act surprised.

"Read the card! Who's it from?" everyone asked all excited.

"I love Nanette and hot chocolate!" read Nanette. Then she looked over at me and said, "See, I knew Angela wasn't his type. Bob loves me!"

That's when the Nin twins, January and Karlene piped up.

"I knew it was only a matter of time before Bob dumped Angela for you!" said one.

"I knew it even before January did!" said the other.

Then everyone in the class, even Mrs Brinks, looked over at me with pity, as Ninnie-Poo poured me a cup of hot chocolate.

"Poor Angela," she said, not meaning it at all. "Perhaps this steaming cup of hot chocolate will help mend your broken heart."

"Don't worry, we still love you and hot chocolate, Angela Anaconda," whispered Gina Lash as she stared at my cup of chocolate.

"Even if you were dumped," added Johnny.

Now, as crazy as it might sound, I started to get mad that my imaginary boyfriend suddenly liked Ninnie Wart and not me.

Chapter 4

"Fine," I think to myself as I stare into my hot chocolate. "She can have him!"

But then, the next thing I know, I start to imagine that time goes backwards and it's morning again and we are playing Mrs Brinks's Unscramble the Scrambled Flashcard Game. Only this time, in my mind, it will be Angela's Unscramble the Scrambled Flashcard Game. And this time, I, Angela Anaconda have a very special pack of cards. One card is my backstabbing flashcard boyfriend Bob and another is a certain baloney curled backstabbing girl. Can you guess who it is? You're right! It is you, Nanette Manoir, the love of Bob's imaginary life. And so, as I shuffle you both into the deck we are ready to play. Look at how flashcard Nin looks lovingly at flashcard Bob. What is the sentence you ask? 'Nanette cannot love anyone but Bob,' you guess. Whoops. I'm afraid that is wrong, Little Nin. The right answer is 'Bob can love anyone, but not Nanette.'

Don't be offended Miss Nin, let's try another. Let me reshuffle the cards. "Bob's love for Nanette rings like a bell," you guess this time? I am so sorry to correct you again Nanette, but that 4 is really a 2 and the correct way to read that sentence is: 'Bob loves to ring Nanette like a bell!' What's that you are screaming? You'd rather not be rung in the belltower like a big giant bell? Never fear Ninnie-Poo, because first comes love, then comes marriage, then comes Bob pushing a baby carriage – just in time to catch you Ninnawatha of the Dimwits as you fall out of the belltower and into the baby carriage pushed by loving card Bob.

Oh dear, you begin to cry. Don't worry Nanette-compoop, even though you are a baby, it does not mean that your relationship will be just a flash in the pan.

Here, let me make a new sentence for you to read: 'Nanette and Bob live happily ever after,' you guess? Oh, sorry, Little Ninny but you are wrong again! Let's rescramble that to the right answer: "After Nanette, Bob lives ever happily." So sorry, Little Nin, I will call as I watch flashcard Bob dump you off a cliff and I hear you screaming. Have a nice trip!

Chapter 5

Just then, I could also hear Mrs Brinks screaming in our classroom which made me forget all about my fun version of Unscramble the Scrambled Flashcard. "My Bob is missing!" Mrs Brinks is screaming. "All right, which one of you hooligans is the culprit?"

Then, you-know-who says: "*Excusez-moi*, Mrs Brinks, but the last person I saw with Bob was Angela Anaconda."

"Open your desk, Angela Anaconda!" Mrs Brinks tells me.

And that's when I discover the torn pieces of her Bob flashcard! Everyone was shocked! Including me! I did not know then what I know now, which is that Johnny

Abatti had ripped up Mrs Brinks' Bob flashcard and thrown him in my desk because he was jealous of Bob.

"Young lady, I demand an explanation!" ordered Mrs Brinks. But I didn't have one! I looked over at Miss Ninnie Wart Manoir who was so happy that I was in trouble, and suddenly I had an idea.

"I ripped up the flash card of Bob because I broke up with Bob!" I answered, figuring I might as well act as crazy as everyone else. I had nothing to lose.

"You broke up?" Johnny Abatti asked, trying to contain his excitement.

"You broke up?" Nanette Manoir asked. Now she was worried.

And then Mrs Brinks started to realize how nutty this had become and said: "You broke up? With a piece of cardboard? Young lady, this time I believe you have truly lost your marbles!"

Instead of sending me to the principal for ripping up her flashcard, Mrs Brinks sent me to the guidance counsellor which is where I guess you go when there's something wrong with your marbles.

"Poor Nanette," I said. "I hope you don't mind being Bob's second choice."

"Second choice?" she shrieked. "I'm not ..." For once Nin the Pin could not find the right words. I was getting good at turning things around.

I was just starting to enjoy my victory when something even crazier happened.

The classroom door opened and a new kid came in. He walked straight over to Mrs Brinks and handed her a piece of paper to read. We couldn't believe our eyes. The new kid looked just like Bob – Bob the flashcard Bob!

"Class," said Mrs Brinks, almost in a whisper, like she was in the middle of a bad dream. "I'd like to introduce you to a new student. His name is ... Bob?"

Now I know people say I have a big imagination, but sometimes true life can be even crazier than the things that even I think up!

I wonder if the real Bob loves hot chocolate? I laughed to myself, as I headed to the guidance counsellor's office.

THE END

"Hi, if you've enjoyed this book, why not read some more books about me, Angela Anaconda, and the other folks at Tapwater Springs. We have a cool selection."

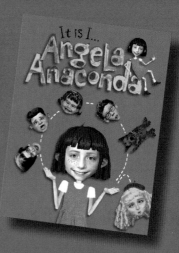

Coming Soon . . .

GORDY RHINEHART'S RAINY DAY ACTIVITY BOOK

SCHOOL IS A NECESSARY EVIL

PIZZA WARS

FLOUR POWER